D1096206

RECEIVED

NOV 15 2019

Douglass-Truth Branch Library

I ~~can't~~ can fly

Fifi Kuo

little bee books

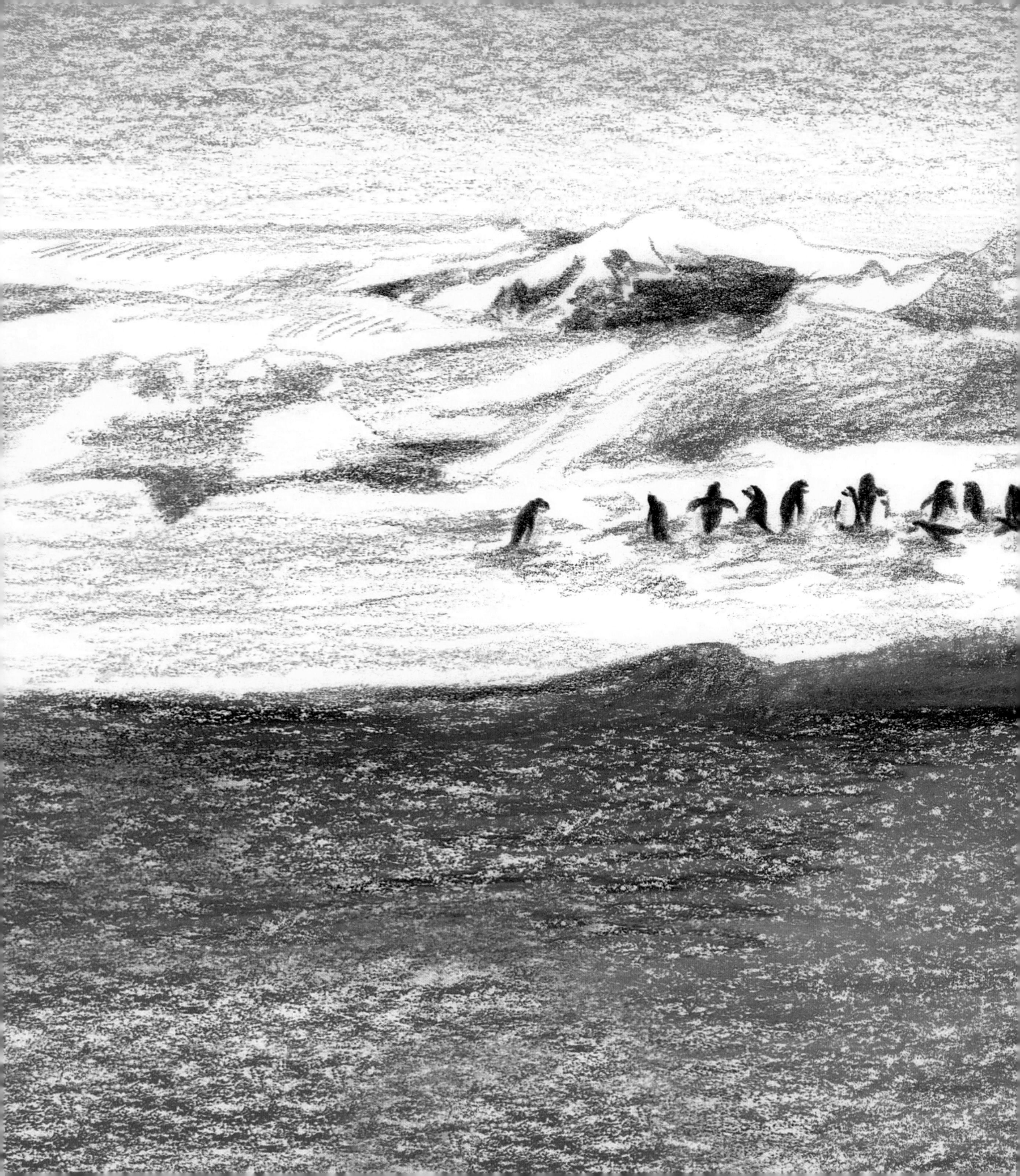

Little Penguin
wanted to fly
like other birds.

"Why can't I fly?" asked Little Penguin.

"Ha!" said Gull. "Penguins CAN'T fly!"

But I DO have wings,
thought Little Penguin.

So Little Penguin flapped.

Then he flapped some more.

And then he flapped *really* hard.

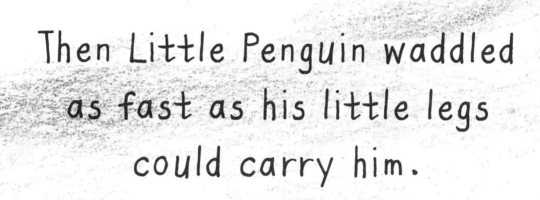

Then Little Penguin waddled
as fast as his little legs
could carry him.

And he leapt....

Whoosh!
Splat!

He landed
in front
of his dad.

"What are you doing, Little Penguin?" asked Dad.

"I want to fly!"
said Little Penguin.

"Like
other
birds."

"Penguins can't fly,"
said Dad.
"Penguins swim."

I'm sure I can fly,
thought Little Penguin.

So Little Penguin flipped and flapped his little wings.

And then he flipped

and flapped some more.

Little Penguin was exhausted.

"I know I can do better,"
said Little Penguin.

Then he slipped

and slipped,

bumped

and tripped,
and . . .

. . . he fell

SPLASH!

into the sea.

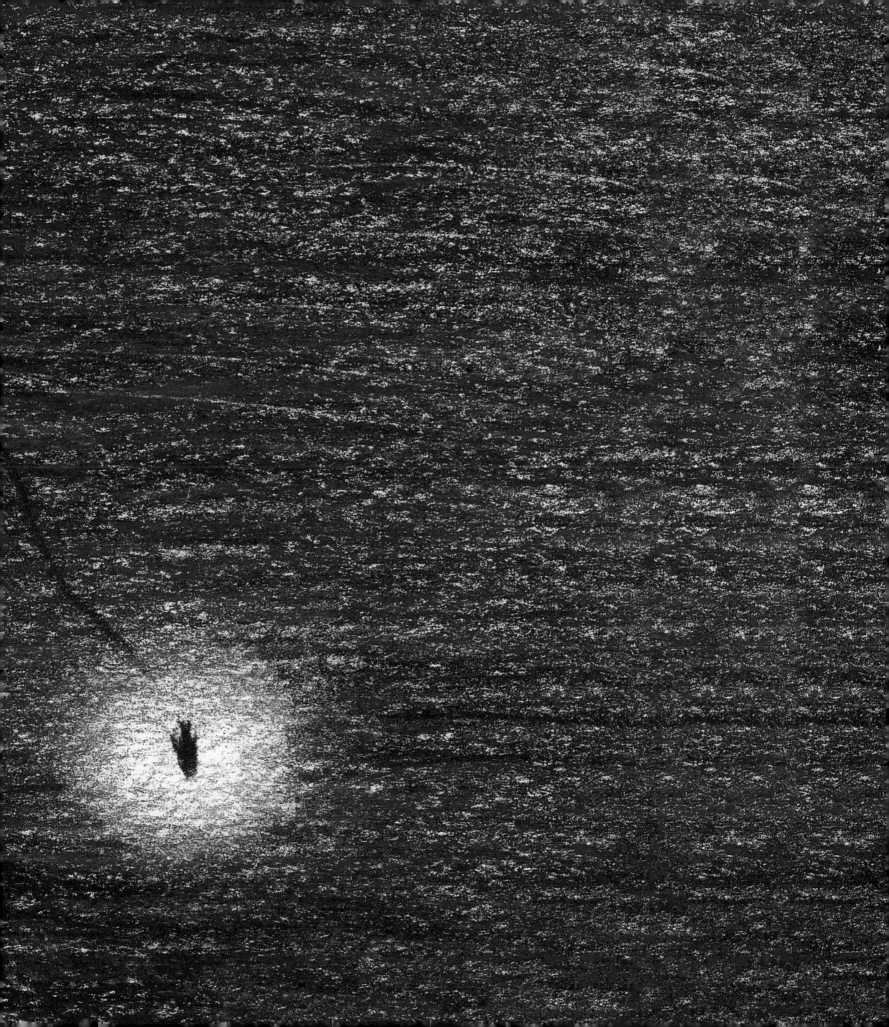

Dad was close by

and he took Little Penguin's wing.

They swam below the sea.
They leapt above the sea.

They flew in the air
and dived again and again.

This is just like flying, thought Little Penguin.

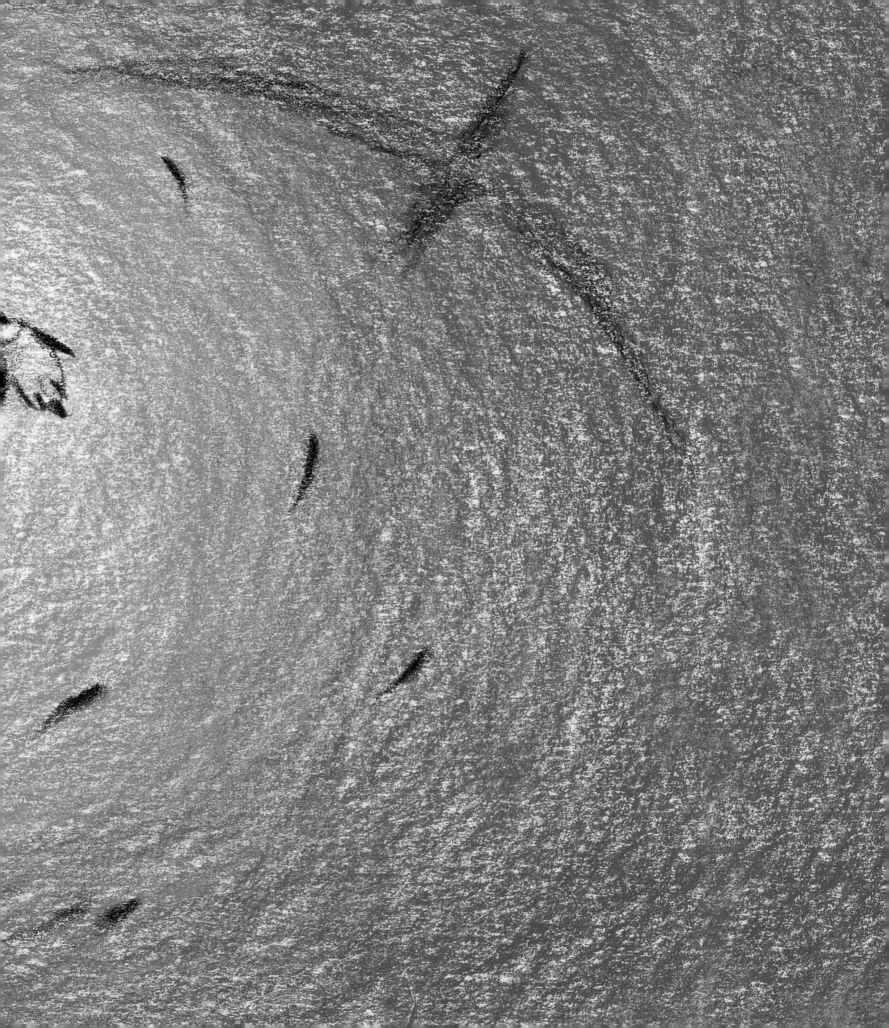

"Swimming is like flying,
isn't it, Dad?"

"Almost the same, my little penguin."

"I can fly!"

This book is for my parents and grandparents,
for giving me the chance to have adventures.
For Martin, Caroline, David, and Leilani,
thanks for believing that I can fly.
Thank you, too, to my godparents in Chung-Li, Hippo, and my friends,
who always cheer me up. And you, the one reading this book.
-FK

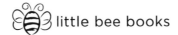 little bee books

An imprint of Bonnier Publishing USA
251 Park Avenue South, New York, NY 10010
Copyright © 2018 by Fifi Kuo
All rights reserved, including the right of reproduction in whole or in part in any form.
Little Bee Books is a trademark of Bonnier Publishing USA,
and associated colophon is a trademark of Bonnier Publishing USA.
Manufactured in China

First published in Great Britain in 2018 by Boxer Books Limited.
First U.S. Edition
2 4 6 8 10 9 7 5 3 1

Library of Congress Cataloging-in-Publication Data is available upon request.
ISBN 978-1-4998-0741-7
littlebeebooks.com
bonnierpublishingusa.com